Diamonds Are Trouble

Books by Scott Corbett

Diamonds Are Trouble

By SCOTT CORBETT

Holt, Rinehart and Winston
NEW YORK CHICAGO SAN FRANCISCO

TO BILL ARBUCKLE
Who reminds me of Ambrose Bunker

1

THE bus disappeared down the highway, leaving Jeff Adams in what looked like the middle of nowhere. Suitcase in hand, he started along the narrow, curving side lane. By now, stars were shining. The air was cool and fresh, and smelled of the sea. He began to enjoy his walk past dark and silent woods. Only twice did he pass houses. Both were dark.

At last the lane met a larger road. Across the road was a driveway. A sign beside it under an old-fashioned lamp said "Westham Inn." Under the name, in smaller letters, was the name of the owner, Ambrose Bunker.

Jeff had talked to Mr. Bunker on the phone. Mr. Bunker needed a summer helper. The helper had to be over twenty-one. Jeff felt sure he would get the job. Pretty sure, anyway.

"Keep your fingers crossed," he told himself, and started up the gravel driveway. Every few yards it was lined with large stones painted white. They shone dimly in the darkness under the trees and bushes.

A piece of gravel flipped into Jeff's shoe. It felt sharp as a knife. Growling to himself, he sat down on a large stone beside a bush.

Taking off his shoe, he dumped out the gravel. Then he sat peering ahead up the driveway. On one side he could see a few small dark buildings. They looked like cottages. Beyond them, lights twinkled through the trees. That was probably the main house.

As he was pulling on his shoe, a movement in the darkness ahead made him glance up again. He saw a black figure slip across the driveway. While he watched, the man came nearer, tiptoeing along. It was too dark to see what he looked like.

He stopped alongside the nearest cottage. Jeff sat still, hidden by his bush. The man turned and went to work on one of the cottage window-screens.

8 .

Slowly he managed to push it up in its slot.

A burglar!

Jeff rose silently to his feet. If he caught a burglar, Mr. Bunker would surely give him the job. He moved carefully forward, keeping off the gravel. His thick-soled shoes were noiseless on the grass. The man was just getting ready to climb in through the window when Jeff pounced on him.

There was a short wrestling-match. Then Jeff was sitting on top of a short, plump, bald man who stared up at him popeyed through round glasses. Sitting on top of him was like sitting on top of a small round hill. The burglar had not been dieting lately. Jeff pinned his arms against the ground.

"All right," growled Jeff, "now let's go see Mr. Bunker."

"What do you mean?" snapped the man. "I *am* Mr. Bunker!"

Jeff's mouth fell open.

"Who are you?" demanded Mr. Bunker, "and what are you doing here?"

"I—er—I'm Jeff Adams. The one who phoned about the summer job."

"What? I didn't expect you till tomorrow!"

"I got a chance for a ride most of the way today, so I came."

9 ·

Mr. Bunker snorted. "Fine thing! Do you usually ask someone for a job while you're sitting on his stomach?"

"No, sir," said Jeff, and hastily got off it. Mr. Bunker stood up and brushed himself off angrily. Jeff's sense of humor got the best of him. He grinned.

"I'll admit, this is an unusual job interview," he said.

"Hah! Well, I certainly don't need a wise guy who jumps me in the dark!"

"Oh, I don't know about that," said Jeff, still amused, and glanced at the open window.

The small plump man's round eyes followed his glance. Then Mr. Bunker drew himself up.

"Now, wait a minute! It's not the way you think!"

But suddenly he realized how things looked. Even in the dark Jeff could tell his face was red.

"Listen, come inside and I'll explain," he snapped. "Wait till I pull this screen down again . . ."

"I'll get my bag," said Jeff, and hurried down the driveway, grinning to himself. Somehow he could not believe Mr. Bunker was a part-time burglar, stealing from his own guests. But at the same time, thought Jeff, I certainly have him in a crack!

2

$\mathcal{W}$HEN Jeff reached the inn, Mr. Bunker was waiting for him at a side entrance. He was patting his bald head with his handkerchief. Obviously he was not used to wrestling.

"What a workout! It's all I can do to get my breath back," he puffed, frowning at Jeff.

The inn was a pleasant, rambling old house. It was painted barn red. It was not large, maybe fifteen rooms.

"After you, sir," said Jeff, and followed Mr. Bunker inside.

Nobody else seemed to be around. The room they had entered was a comfortable sitting room. The ceiling beams were only a few inches above Jeff's head. There was a bar in one corner. It was the kind of room guests would enjoy sitting around in, having a drink.

The two men looked each other over. Mr. Bunker saw a tall, rangy young man with a firm mouth and steady eyes. Jeff saw a small round man who seemed to be feeling better, now that he could see what Jeff looked like.

"Want a drink?" asked Mr. Bunker.

"No, sir, but I could use some coffee."

"Okay. After what you put me through, I'll have both. Come along."

A door beside the bar led into the kitchen. A coffeepot was sitting on the big electric stove.

"Coffee's already hot. Grab a couple of cups over there."

He watched the quick, efficient way Jeff moved. Jeff took cups and saucers from a shelf and brought them to the stove. He knew he was being watched, and why. Mr. Bunker looked satisfied. He filled the cups. Jeff carried them into the sitting room without slopping into the saucers. Mr. Bunker poured himself a brandy, and they sat down.

"How old are you, Jeff?"

"Twenty-two, sir. After high school I did my army service. Now I'm in college. I'll finish next year."

"Good for you. So you're a friend of Freddie's."

"Yes, sir. He was really sorry to let you down at the last minute. Especially after working for you last summer. That's why he called me. He knew my summer job had folded up unexpectedly, and I was looking for something else."

Jeff had told him most of this before, on the phone. But Mr. Bunker had seemed distracted at the time. Jeff thought he had better say it again.

Mr. Bunker nodded.

"So that's the story, eh? Well, cheers," he said, and tipped up his glass. "Ah! I needed that."

He settled himself in his chair.

"Well, now. The thing that's causing the trouble around here is a diamond necklace. Mrs. Walling's diamond necklace."

Mr. Bunker sighed.

"Mrs. Walling is my best customer. We're old friends. She spends part of the summer here every year. She's amusing, she's rich, she's generous, she's good company. But in one way, this year, she's driving me crazy."

"How's that, sir?"

"Well, she has a diamond necklace. The stones in it look the size of hens' eggs. I can hardly sleep nights, worrying about someone stealing it."

"Well, I can help you out there," began Jeff, but Mr. Bunker held up his hand.

"Wait a minute. You haven't heard the worst. You haven't heard about Mr. Wolfe."

Mr. Bunker stopped for another sip of brandy. He looked as if Mr. Wolfe's name left a bad taste in his mouth.

"A few days ago Mr. Augustus V. Wolfe checked in," he went on. "He came driving up in a big sedan and rented a cottage for two weeks. Big smooth fat man dressed in expensive, well-tailored clothes. Right away he bothered me. I didn't like the way he looked at Mrs. Walling's necklace. Like it gave him itchy palms. He said he used to be in the furniture business, but had retired. He gave a Chicago address as his home."

Mr. Bunker finished off his brandy.

"Now then. There aren't many guests here yet, this early in the season. Besides Mrs. Walling and Wolfe, only three others. So tonight she and Wolfe went to the movies, and the other three went off to visit some friends in the village. I had the place to myself."

Jeff took a sip of coffee. That reminded Mr. Bunker that he had some, too. He swallowed a big gulp of it.

"Well, just on a hunch," he continued, "I went to the telephone and dialed Information in Chicago. I gave Wolfe's name and address, and asked for his telephone number."

Mr. Bunker paused.

"There was no Augustus V. Wolfe listed at that address in Chicago. That address, or any other."

They stared at each other.

"Now, Wolfe looks like a man who would have his own telephone at home. And yet . . ."

"In other words, Mr. Bunker, it all seems suspicious, but you haven't proved anything yet."

"That's right. So next, I decided to have a look in Wolfe's cottage while everybody was away. Maybe I could find some evidence he's a phony. He's probably too smart for that, but still, you never can tell. Even smart crooks make stupid mistakes."

An annoyed look crossed Mr. Bunker's round face.

"I should talk about mistakes, though! I swear, it's just not my night. First off, I started across the side lawn in the dark. Well, somebody had forgotten to pull up one croquet wicket. I caught my foot in it and flopped down hard. The key to Wolfe's cottage went flying out of my hand. When I got up, I couldn't find it anywhere."

Jeff kept his face straight, but his eyes were enjoying themselves. He could not help imagining how Mr. Bunker looked, flopping down on the lawn.

Mr. Bunker glared at him. Then the plump man grinned sourly. Finally they both laughed.

"All right," said Mr. Bunker. "So now I was getting stubborn. I was going to have a look around in Wolfe's cabin, even if I had to climb in the window. I knew one of his window-screen catches didn't work right."

"I'll fix it tomorrow," said Jeff. "And so then you started to climb in the window, when some wise guy jumped you."

Mr. Bunker grinned again, just as sourly.

"Exactly. And that's the story."

Jeff thought a moment. Then he looked at his watch.

"When does the movie get out?"

"Not for another hour."

"How about the other three guests?"

"They said they'd be late."

They eyed each other silently for a few seconds.

"Well, then," said Jeff, "what are we waiting for?"

"Jeff," said Mr. Bunker, "you're hired. Let's go!"

3

$\mathcal{J}$EFF set his back against the cottage wall and laced his fingers together.

"Here, sir, put your foot in my hands. Might as well do it the easy way."

"Thanks."

"I'd be glad to climb in for you, but you know better what to look for."

"Right."

Jeff was surprised at himself. He had not been at the Westham Inn half an hour. Yet here he was, getting ready to boost his boss through a guest's cottage window! This was not the kind of summer work he had expected to be doing.

A couple of grunts from each of them, and Mr.

Bunker was through the window. Turning on a light, he went to work. Jeff stood guard outside.

The night was still and clear. Somewhere not far away a dog barked. The only other sound was the purr of a car going by on the road below the inn. Now and then Jeff glanced through the window to see how Mr. Bunker was doing.

First he opened the clothes closet and looked around inside it. Next he opened a suitcase and was carefully feeling around in it. Especially in the side pockets.

"Find anything yet?"

Mr. Bunker stopped to look at something.

"Well, maybe . . ."

Then Jeff heard another car. He turned to listen.

No question about it. The car was slowing down out on the road. He whirled back to the window.

"Lights out!" he hissed. "Car coming!"

Mr. Bunker gave him a startled look, then snapped off the light. Blackness.

"Whoever it is, keep them away from here!" he whispered frantically. "I've got to close this suitcase and straighten things up. Then I'll get out as fast as I can. But the door doesn't have a snap lock on it. I'll have to climb back out through the window. So give me plenty of time!"

Car lights showed through the trees, turning into the driveway. Jeff ran for the house like a rabbit. Maybe it was the three guests coming back from the village. Were they staying in the main house or in a cottage? Mr. Bunker had not said.

Not far from the house was an open space for parking. The car pulled into it and stopped. By then Jeff was standing beside the circle drive in front of the inn. The circle was lighted by a handsome lamp on a post.

The car was a big, showy sedan. There were only two people in it. The driver struggled out and waddled around to open the door for his companion. Jeff's heart did a flip. Even in the semi-darkness it was easy to see what the driver looked like. He was a fat man dressed in expensive, well-tailored clothes.

Jeff's legs were shaking as he walked toward the car. The man was helping a lady out. The lamp on the post was a hundred feet away, but its soft glow made something glitter around her neck.

"I'll take this stuff down to my cottage and be right back," said the fat man.

"Good evening," said Jeff.

"Oh!" cried the lady in a high, crackly voice. "You scared me!"

"I'm sorry, ma'am, I didn't mean to. I'm Jeff

Adams, Mr. Bunker's new summer help. You must be Mrs. Walling."

"That's right, and this is Mr. Wolfe."

"How do you do, Mr. Wolfe?"

Mr. Wolfe's reply was a grunt. He opened the rear door of the car. "Give me a hand with this box," he ordered impatiently.

"Yes, sir! If you'll give me your key, I'll be glad to put it in your cottage for you," said Jeff eagerly. Anything to keep Wolfe away from the cottage!

But Wolfe spoiled this plan.

"No, I'll go with you. I'll be right back, Myra."

"Take your time, Gus."

Mrs. Walling walked away toward the house.

"That's half a case of champagne," said Wolfe, "so handle it with care."

Being as slow about it as he could, Jeff hauled the heavy box out of the car.

"Come on, hurry up!" growled Wolfe. "I have to go to the bathroom!"

"Oh! Yes, sir!" said Jeff, and followed him as he began to waddle briskly down the gravel drive toward his cottage.

Jeff's heart was in his mouth now. How could he be sure Mr. Bunker was out of the cottage yet? What if something had delayed him? Come what may, he must slow down Wolfe somehow!

Not only was Wolfe heading straight for his cottage, but he was going the most dangerous way. Obviously he would walk around it on the side where the window was. The other side was blocked by bushes.

It was time for desperate measures. There was only one way Jeff could think of to stop Wolfe. What if he pretended to stumble, and dropped the heavy box on Wolfe's toes?

That ought to do it!

Then, instead of going on to his cottage, Wolfe would probably stamp back to the inn to yell his head off to Mr. Bunker. Of course, Mr. Bunker would have to fire Jeff, but that could not be helped. This was no time to worry about details. Maybe Jeff could come back after Wolfe left.

They had nearly reached the cottage. Jeff was getting up his nerve to drop the box. Suddenly, from up ahead, came a strange, startling noise. A sort of ripping sound.

Jeff thought quickly. Instantly he set down the box and threw out an arm to halt Wolfe.

"What was that?" cried Wolfe. He sounded uneasy. Like a man who was not used to the country.

"That's a skunk," said Jeff. "An angry skunk sometimes makes a sound just like that. Stand absolutely still, sir, and let me have a look first."

"Okay, go ahead!"

Wolfe sounded scared stiff now. Obviously he loved his expensive, well-tailored clothes. He did not want to take them off and bury them. And one thing was certain, *something* was stirring in the grass around the corner. He could hear it.

Carefully Jeff tiptoed ahead and peered around the side of the cottage. Something was just disappearing around the other corner, but it was not a skunk. Jeff relaxed, and then tensed again.

The window-screen was still pushed up!

Glancing back, he held up his hand warningly to Wolfe. Then he slipped around the corner out of sight and reached for the screen.

"Go on, beat it! Get away from here!" he shouted noisily, to cover the sound as he eased down the screen. This done, he returned and signaled Wolfe. The fat man was still frozen to the spot where he had left him.

"All clear, sir. He took off."

"You're sure?"

"Yes, sir. I saw him go."

Wolfe followed Jeff nervously, hurrying along the side of the cottage and around to the door. While he was unlocking it, Jeff went back for the box. Lights snapped on, the screen door slammed. Jeff returned.

"Where shall I put the champagne, sir?"

"Just leave it on the table," Wolfe called from the bathroom.

"Yes, sir."

Jeff set the box down and left. He hurried through the dark toward the inn, walking along a path between the cottages. Pulling out his handkerchief, he wiped beads of sweat off his brow. Now he knew how Mr. Bunker had felt.

"Whew!" he muttered.

A new sound startled him.

"Psst!"

He stopped.

"Jeff!"

He saw a dark form in the bushes.

"Sir?" he whispered.

"Jeff! Listen, I ripped my pants climbing out the window!"

"Oh! Was that the noise we heard?"

"Yes, dammit! You'll have to go in and sneak another pair out to me."

"If Mrs. Walling asks where you are, what shall I say?"

"Tell her—well, tell her I'm out looking for Ruby."

"Ruby?"

"The dog."

"Oh. Yes, sir."

Mr. Bunker clapped a hand to his forehead.

"Good Lord! I left the screen up!"

"I pulled it down."

"Ah!" said Mr. Bunker gratefully.

Quickly he explained where his room was on the second floor. He described a pair of gray slacks hanging in the closet.

"Sneak them out to me somehow!"

"Why don't you sneak over under the window, sir, and I'll drop them out to you?"

"Hm! Why didn't I think of that? Go ahead. I'll be there!"

4

W<small>HEN</small> Jeff entered the small sitting room, Mrs. Walling was standing behind the bar mixing drinks. Her necklace lived up to advance notices. He felt as if he needed dark glasses. He had never seen such big diamonds with so much glitter.

Mrs. Walling was sixty years old if she was a day, but she had flaming red hair. Her face was long, and horsy, but her blue eyes were still young. They had as much sparkle in them as her diamonds, and that was plenty. She had a devil-may-care way about her that was entertaining. She was not afraid to have fun, and she didn't care what anybody thought.

She looked up when Jeff came in, and smiled.

"Well! Is the champagne safe and sound?"

"Yes, Mrs. Walling."

"Where's Mr. Bunker?"

Before Jeff could reply, a dog barked outside and scratched at the screen door.

"That's Ruby. Let her in, will you, Jeff?"

"Er—yes, ma'am. Mr. Bunker's out looking for her."

"Oh, is he? Well, let her in and then find Mr. Bunker and tell him she's here, will you?"

"Yes, ma'am."

He opened the door, and the big boxer rushed in, wagging her stubby tail. There was nothing for Jeff to do now but go outside and pretend to look for Mr. Bunker.

"Mr. Bunker!" he called loudly, and walked around the side of the house. He was passing a bush when he heard a familiar sound.

"Psst!"

"Yes, sir," he whispered.

"What are you doing out here? Where's my pants?"

Jeff explained. Mr. Bunker groaned.

"That silly dog! She would show up at the wrong time! Never mind. Sneak in the front door, and go upstairs that way. But quietly, so Mrs. Walling won't hear you."

Leaving Mr. Bunker behind his bush, Jeff hurried on to the front door. It was not used very much. Easing it open, Jeff slipped inside and up the front stairs like an Indian.

A minute later he was on his way down again with a pair of gray slacks. They were obviously Mr. Bunker's size around the middle. He took them outside, where the waiting man quickly slipped them on. He rolled up his ripped slacks and hid them under the bush. Then he heaved a sigh of relief.

"Wow! Okay, let's go in," he whispered.

"We can even stop whispering," Jeff pointed out.

"Say, that's right."

Footsteps crunched on the gravel of the driveway.

"Here comes Mr. Wolfe," said Jeff, whispering again.

They waited till he had gone inside the house. Then they walked around to the door.

"I found Mr. Bunker," Jeff called in brightly, and opened the door for him.

"You naughty girl," said Mr. Bunker, shaking a finger at Ruby and trying not to glare at her. "Where were you?"

He said hello to Mrs. Walling and Wolfe. They were just sitting down with their drinks.

"What are you two doing back so early?" he asked.

"Oh, the movie was so bad we walked out on it," said Mrs. Walling. "How about a drink, Ambrose?"

"I could use one," admitted Mr. Bunker.

"Brandy, sir?" asked Jeff.

"Brandy," he agreed.

"Say! He knows you already," observed Mrs. Walling.

Jeff went behind the bar. He poured a brandy into a big snifter glass and brought it to his new boss.

"Thank you, Jeff." Mr. Bunker turned to the others. "You've both met Jeff, I suppose? Good."

Wolfe sat bulging in an armchair holding his drink on his large belly in one fat fist. He gave most of his attention to Mrs. Walling. He looked at her a good deal. When he did, his eyes seemed to reflect the bright glitter of her necklace. But he had a smooth, smiling face. Without looking exactly jolly, he managed to seem good-natured and sociable.

Jeff went behind the bar and passed the time straightening up things there.

"Well, our trip tonight wasn't completely wasted," said Wolfe. "I ran into a good buy in champagne at that big liquor store in the shopping center. Tomorrow night at dinner, the champagne will be on me."

The champagne was nearly on you tonight, thought Jeff. A mental picture of glass breaking and champagne fizzing all over the lawn made him shudder. It scared him now to remember how close he had come to dropping the box on Wolfe's toes.

Presently Mr. Bunker finished his brandy and stood up.

"Well, come on, Jeff, you might as well get settled. Grab your bag, and I'll show you where your room is. It's out in the barn."

"In the hayloft," said Mrs. Walling.

"It is not," said Mr. Bunker. "It's a darn nice room, as you'll see."

Jeff got his bag and said good night to the others.

"Watch out for the field mice," said Mrs. Walling. She obviously loved to tease Mr. Bunker.

The barn was only a few yards away behind the house. It was small, and in good condition. Half of it was used for storage. The other half had been made into a plain but comfortable bedroom. It even had a bathroom complete with a shower.

"Looks fine, sir."

"Freddie liked it."

Mr. Bunker shut the door, and immediately they dropped their voices.

"Did you find out anything, sir?"

"Not much, Jeff. I wish I'd had more time. Still, there were a couple of interesting things. First of all, his clothes."

"You looked at the labels?"

"Yes."

"Were they Chicago?"

"No. Los Angeles, all of them. Of course, that doesn't prove a thing, either, but still . . . There was a monogrammed handkerchief in one jacket, but the monogram was 'W.' The most interesting thing I found was a packet of business cards in the side pocket of his suitcase. His name was printed on them, 'Augustus V. Wolfe,' and under his name, 'Appraisals.' "

"Appraisals?"

"Yes. That would usually mean someone who goes around appraising estates, or doing insurance appraisals. An appraiser goes in and looks at everything in a house, and decides how much each thing is worth."

"But he says he was in the furniture business, and has retired."

"Well, it's still possible he could do appraisals

now and then, in a part-time way. He could also be a phony who uses the cards to get in places. Who knows?"

"He would have to know something about the value of things," said Jeff.

"Such as jewels," said Mr. Bunker.

"Such as jewels," nodded Jeff.

They eyed each other thoughtfully. Then Mr. Bunker sat down on the bed and groaned in a put-upon way.

"I wish Myra Walling would leave that necklace of hers at home!"

"Does she wear it all the time?"

"No, only in the evenings—but it's almost worse when she's *not* wearing it. At least, when she has it on, I know where it is!"

He shrugged his round shoulders.

"Well, get yourself settled, and have a good night's sleep. You're off to a good start around here. I don't mind saying so—tonight you earned whatever I'm going to pay you. We'll talk about that to-morrow."

Out came his handkerchief again. Once again he mopped his shiny bald head. Its splendid glitter almost rivaled Mrs. Walling's diamond necklace.

"What a night! I told you it wasn't my night. I've tripped over a wicket and flopped on the lawn. I've been jumped by a wise guy. I've almost been caught climbing out a guest's cottage window. And I've ripped my pants doing it. I'm aching in every muscle," he said, groaning as he stood up. "Why, I've even been called a skunk! I'm going to bed! Good night!"

5

Mr. Bunker called him at six. Jeff quickly shaved and dressed and joined his boss in the kitchen. While they had a cup of coffee, Mr. Bunker explained how the inn was run.

"Two local women come in to clean the rooms and the cottages, and one helps in the kitchen. I do the cooking myself."

Jeff's job was to wait table, mow the lawns, help wash up the dishes, and do an occasional odd job. The salary Mr. Bunker offered was good.

While they were talking, Jeff glanced out the window. Suddenly he jumped up.

"Look!"

Ruby came romping into sight on the lawn. She was carrying a pair of slacks. She shook them gaily above her head.

"Oh, my gosh, I forgot about those," cried Mr. Bunker, and rushed outside, followed by Jeff.

"Ruby!" he called sternly, but in a low voice, so as not to wake the guests. "Come here this minute!"

But Ruby wanted to make a game of it. They had to chase her around the lawn. Jeff glanced anxiously toward the house, and toward Wolfe's cottage. It would be bad if the guests learned that their host had ripped a pair of slacks. Wolfe just might remember that strange sound he heard the night before.

"Ruby! Drop those! Drop them at once!" ordered her master.

But Ruby had not received much obedience training. Mr. Bunker was not built for running, but he ran anyway, getting madder by the minute. All at once he did a belly flop on the lawn. Ruby was so surprised she stopped to look. Jeff snatched the slacks away from her.

Still lying on the lawn, Mr. Bunker looked back at his foot and swore.

"That same damn wicket!"

"Hold it!" cried Jeff. "Hold the position. Now,

let's see. If you had a key in your hand, it ought to
fly in this direction . . ."

Stooping along, nose close to the ground, Jeff inspected the lawn.

"Here it is, sir!"

Leaning on his elbow, Mr. Bunker looked disgusted.

"Nothing like finding a key the hard way!"

The first people down for breakfast were the three
who had been visiting friends in the village the
night before. They were a couple called Haney,
and Mr. Haney's mother.

"The old lady knits and does crossword puzzles.
The Haneys watch birds," Mr. Bunker told him.
"They're no trouble. They love my food."

After a while Wolfe came in, and before he had
started to eat Mrs. Walling joined him. Wolfe ate
four fried eggs and half a pound of bacon. Mrs.
Walling had black coffee and two strips of dry toast,
and three cigarettes in a long ivory holder.

She was not wearing her necklace at that hour. In
some ways she looked better when it was not there
to compete with her snapping blue eyes. She
laughed and joked, and teased Mr. Bunker by pretending to complain about everything.

After a while she went to her room and came back waving a printed notice.

"What about this auction Friday, Ambrose?" she asked. "The Collins estate. Is it going to be a good one?"

"Of course. Because I'm doing the catering at the refreshments stand. Sandwiches, cake, and plenty of my wonderful coffee—"

"Never mind the bad food, what about the sale? It says there will be Colonial furniture, silverware, jewelry, paintings, a tractor lawnmower, an automatic dishwasher—"

"I'm thinking of bidding on the dishwasher," said Mr. Bunker.

"A country auction, eh?" said Wolfe. "I haven't been to one of those in years."

"Not exactly a country auction," said Mr. Bunker. "Colonel Collins had some nice things in his house. Odd man, though. He lived alone in a big house on a back lane over in the village. Regular hermit. Then he died suddenly of a heart attack, which must have been more of a surprise to him than anybody. He always told everybody he never had a sick day in his life."

"When did he die?" asked Mrs. Walling.

"About two months ago. His only relatives were

two sisters in Omaha. They didn't want most of his things, so they're holding this auction."

A car came racing up the driveway. Mr. Bunker paused to look out the window.

"If you want to know any more about it, here's your chance," he said. "Here comes Hadley Ransom now."

"Oh, good," said Mrs. Walling. "He's the auctioneer."

"You must come to the auction," Mrs. Walling told Wolfe. "Hadley is something to watch when he's running one. He can hold up an ugly vase and ask, 'How much am I bid for this fine old French vase?' and make you feel it's worth buying. 'Do I hear five dollars? Five dollars! Who will bid six? I have six dollars!' And before he's through, he'll get somebody to bid ten for it!"

The car slid to a stop, shooting gravel onto the lawn. Hadley Ransom blew into the house, tall, noisy, and important, a walking advertisement for his business.

"My first auction of the season, and a fine one," he boasted, after he had been introduced. He sat down at the breakfast table and accepted a cup of coffee. "Come over to my place tomorrow morning and you'll see. Lots of good things. They're so good we're allowing two days before the sale for people to look at everything, to see what they want to bid on."

Hadley Ransom paused until everyone looked at him. Then he lowered his voice in a confidential way.

"In fact, I've just had an exciting phone call. Jason Brown of the Boston Museum is coming down tomorrow for a look."

"Jason Brown?"

Wolfe's voice was sharp as he repeated the name. Then just as quickly he recovered himself, and was smooth and smiling again.

"He's curator of the American Wing of the museum. Do you know him?" asked Ransom.

"Oh, no. I was thinking of another man."

"Have you any idea what he may be interested in, Hadley?" asked Mrs. Walling. The auctioneer shook his head.

"No idea. Though if you ask me, it should be the Colonial cupboard. That's a real museum piece."

He and Mr. Bunker discussed details about the refreshments for the day of the auction. Then he rushed away again.

After a while Jeff went to work on the side lawn, mowing and trimming. There was plenty of lawn to work on. At one end it stretched to the edge of a steep slope overlooking a lake. From the other end

Jeff could catch a glimpse of salt marshes and the sea. A brook ran from the lake down through the marshes to the sea. Several seagulls were circling around over the brook. Jeff took a deep breath of the clean air and thought about how pleasant it would be to go to the beach. But it was pleasant to work in the sunshine high on a hill, too. He was enjoying himself when his boss appeared.

"How's it going, Jeff?"

"Fine, sir."

Mr. Bunker lowered his voice.

"Wolfe made a phone call to Boston. He just paid me for it. He must have gone into the front of the house and used the extension there, so that none of us would hear."

"Hmm. Boston. Did you notice how he acted when Mr. Ransom mentioned that man at the museum?"

"Jason Brown?" Mr. Bunker nodded thoughtfully. "Yes, I noticed."

"I think that name meant something to him, don't you, sir?"

Again Mr. Bunker nodded.

"But I can't imagine what connection that could have with—with anything, Jeff. I'll admit, I can't figure this Wolfe character out. I simply have this feeling he's not on the level."

Later in the morning a Mr. Tuttle called from Boston to reserve a cottage. He said he would be driven down to the inn that afternoon.

"Well?" said Mr. Bunker to Jeff, after he had hung up. "Is it a coincidence, or isn't it?"

6

WHO was Mr. Tuttle? Did he have any connection with Wolfe's call to Boston? Why had Wolfe seemed concerned when Jason Brown's name was mentioned?

Mr. Pierpont Tuttle showed up at four in the afternoon. He arrived in a chauffeur-driven rented car. He stepped out, a small, prissy, elderly man, and stood blinking around him in the sunshine.

"Very pleasant. Very pleasant indeed. I think I shall like it here. Mr. Bunker? Oh, yes, how do you do?" he said in a dry, precise voice, shaking hands with his host. Jeff took his bag from the chauffeur.

Mr. Tuttle himself was carrying a neat leather dispatch case.

"May I take your case, sir?" asked Jeff.

But Mr. Tuttle kept it.

"Thank you, I am used to carrying it myself," he said in a fussy manner. "Which one is to be my cottage?"

"This way, Mr. Tuttle," said Mr. Bunker, and led him to the cottage next to Wolfe's. Mr. Tuttle inspected it.

"Yes, yes, this will do nicely. I am very much in need of a rest. Your inn has been highly recommended to me. At what time is dinner served?"

"At seven."

"Very good. I shall get myself settled, and then take a nap."

Jeff and Mr. Bunker returned to the inn.

"One good thing," said Jeff, "even if there is anything to be suspicious about, they have no reason to think we *are* suspicious of them."

"That's right. And let's keep it that way. Let's be very careful not to seem nosy."

"Right, sir."

Mr. Bunker's eyes twinkled behind their round glasses.

"But that doesn't mean we shouldn't keep on *being* nosy," he added.

At five thirty the guests began to gather in the small sitting room. The Haneys appeared. Jeff poured three sherries for them from their bottle. The inn did not have a license to serve liquor. Instead, the guests brought their own. Mr. Bunker furnished whatever set-ups were needed—ice, soda, ginger ale, or water.

Mrs. Walling appeared. She fixed drinks for herself, Wolfe, and Mr. Bunker. Wolfe showed up carrying three bottles of champagne to be put on ice for dinner.

"Champagne for everybody tonight!" he announced with great good humor.

Quick, precise steps rattled the gravel outside. Jeff tried not to watch too obviously as the door opened and Mr. Tuttle entered.

"Good evening," said Mr. Bunker. He stood up and introduced the newcomer to everybody. Jeff watched closely when they came to Wolfe.

The two men seemed to be meeting for the first time. They shook hands briefly, and showed no more than polite interest in each other. They acted like strangers who wanted to be agreeable. Wolfe asked Mr. Tuttle what he did.

"I have investments in several firms," said Mr. Tuttle in his dry voice. "It keeps me rather busy. I plan to retire soon."

All six guests seemed to enjoy dinner thoroughly that night. Wolfe's champagne added a lot to their pleasure. Old Mrs. Haney said the bubbles tickled her nose, but she did not let that stop her from having two glasses. Wolfe had four or five. Mr. Tuttle made do with one.

They talked about the Collins auction.

"I'm not sure I approve of auctions," said Mr. Tuttle. "Most people seem to buy things they don't really need."

"Still, you shouldn't miss the fun," said Mrs. Walling. Her blue eyes sparkled at Mr. Tuttle. "And I'm sure you're a man of much too strong character to bid on anything you don't need. Besides, tomorrow morning isn't the auction. Tomorrow we're only going to look at the things that will be for sale."

Mr. Tuttle's thin lips curled into a small smile, and he coughed behind his hand.

"Well, I suppose I might as well go along in the morning," he said. "It won't hurt to have a look."

The others laughed, and Mrs. Walling said, "That's the spirit!"

She was wearing her necklace, as usual. Jeff watched to see if Mr. Tuttle took any special notice of it. He did not seem to. He spoke to Mrs. Walling now and then, but no more than to the others. For that matter, he did not talk a great deal. Wolfe and Mrs. Walling did most of the talking.

After dinner the guests and Mr. Bunker were back in the sitting room when the telephone rang. It was a call from Boston for Mr. Tuttle. When he came to the telephone, all conversation stopped, so that he could hear.

"Yes? Oh, yes, Marshall. What? Tomorrow? At what time? Two o'clock? Oh, drat it!" Mr. Tuttle sounded annoyed. "Is a meeting absolutely necessary at this time? If you ask me, Harrison is getting to be an old woman about these things . . . Well, if we must, we must, I suppose. Very well. Tell them I shall be there."

He hung up and returned to his chair, looking disgusted.

"Just when I hoped for a good rest!"

"What's the matter, Mr. Tuttle?"

"Oh, I have to go back to Boston for a board meeting. I shall have to hire a car tomorrow morning to drive me up and back."

"That sounds like an awful nuisance," said Wolfe. He thought a moment, and then sat forward. "Tell you what. Let's all take in the auction display in the morning, and then I'll run you up to Boston in my car. Maybe Mrs. Walling will go with us."

He turned to her.

"If you will, I'll take you to lunch at the best French restaurant in town."

"Now, that sounds worthwhile," said Mrs. Walling, her eyes bright. "I'd love to go."

"Well, I must say, that's most kind of you, Mr. Wolfe," said Mr. Tuttle. "You're sure it will be convenient?"

"Why not? It's a good excuse for a spree, eh, Mrs. Walling?"

Jeff was careful not to glance at Mr. Bunker while all this was going on. But he wondered what he was thinking.

A few minutes later Mr. Bunker came to the bar.

"You can call it a night, Jeff."

"All right, sir. Thank you."

Jeff had not been in his room long before he heard Mr. Bunker outside calling Ruby. Then there was a tap on his door. He opened it. Mr. Bunker slipped inside.

"Well, Jeff, what do you think about this latest development? Those two, getting Mrs. Walling to drive to Boston with them! I don't like it one little bit!"

Before Jeff could reply, there was a scratch at the door, and a whine from Ruby. Mr. Bunker pulled open the door.

"Oh, Ruby, stop that! If I really wanted you, you

wouldn't come for fifteen minutes! Get in here before you attract attention!"

Ruby romped in and jumped up on both of them, licking them affectionately.

"Down! Sit!"

After Ruby had finally settled down, Jeff said, "It really does sound as if they're up to something. Do you think you ought to warn Mrs. Walling, and stop her from going?"

Mr. Bunker threw up his hands.

"Only as a last resort. Frankly, I hate to tell her anything about our suspicions. You never know what she's likely to say or do. And even now, we could be wrong about the whole business. Supposing we were. Supposing we were wrong, and she said something to Wolfe that gave us away. It would be terribly embarrassing."

Mr. Bunker squirmed unhappily.

"Besides, I couldn't tell her about our suspicions without telling her everything. And I'd hate to tell her about climbing through Wolfe's window, and all that. I'd never hear the end of it! I can hear her laughing now!"

"That's for sure," Jeff agreed. "I guess all we can do is wait till tomorrow. Maybe we can come up with some way to head her off without telling her anything."

Mr. Bunker nodded.

"I'm going to wait till the last minute," he said grimly. "Maybe we'll find out something before it's time for them to leave tomorrow. Maybe something will happen to change her mind about going."

He rose to his feet.

"But if it doesn't, I'm going to take her aside and tell her everything. Even if it means making a fool of myself, I'm going to tell her. I'm not going to let her leave here with those two!"

7

"I WANT to see the Collins stuff myself," said Mr. Bunker next morning, when the guests were at breakfast. "Jeff, you can come too, if you want. When the auction is on, you and I won't have a chance to watch. We'll be busy at the refreshments stand."

"Think it's going to rain?" asked Wolfe.

The sky was gray and gloomy. Mr. Bunker took a look at it.

"It might," he said, "but I doubt it. Not soon, anyway."

"It feels like rain to me," said Mr. Tuttle. "At

any rate, I shall certainly take along my raincoat.
And I advise the rest of you to do the same. Better
safe than sorry, I always say."

Before long they were all in the big tent behind
Hadley Ransom's house. The tent was decorated
with gay pennants. It looked large enough to hold a
circus. All the side flaps were rolled up a foot or
two to let in air and light.

When the auction was on, the tent would hold
rows of chairs for the public. Now it was filled with
pieces of furniture, household equipment, rolled-up
rugs, and long tables on which the smaller articles
were displayed.

As usual, Mr. Bunker was nervous about Mrs.
Walling. She was not wearing her diamond necklace.

"That crazy woman has it in her purse. I know she
has," he growled under his breath to Jeff. "Keep an
eye on her. I'd hate to have some purse-snatcher
grab her bag."

Jeff was able to watch her and still look at all the
things that were going to be sold. He was amazed at
how many different articles were displayed. Just
about everything he could think of seemed to be in-
cluded.

He looked at the Colonial cupboard Hadley Ransom said was good enough to be in a museum. He

looked at tables, chairs, vases, pictures, glassware, fishing rods, and books. He saw an old-style phonograph that looked as if *it* ought to be in a museum. He looked at the automatic dishwasher Mr. Bunker said he might bid on.

Half a dozen old pictures, behind glass in small frames, were hung on a board. Their glass gave him a perfect reflection of Mrs. Walling, across the tent. For a while he looked at the pictures and kept an eye on her at the same time.

The tent was crowded with people. Most of them were summer people. There were all kinds. Men in loud sports shirts and shorts. Women in big straw hats and all sorts of slacks and beach costumes. There were even a few pretty girls in the crowd. Jeff found them more interesting than most of the display. Maybe he would meet some of them on the beach later.

Hadley Ransom was moving about the tent greeting everybody. He was pleased because so many people had come.

"It will be too bad if it rains," said Jeff.

"Not at all," said the auctioneer. "A little rain will keep people off the beach. They'll come here instead."

Mr. Bunker had been making a round of the tent. He joined them now.

"Lots of interest in this auction, Ambrose," said Ransom. "You'll sell a ton of food."

"I hope so, Hadley. By the way, when will that museum man be showing up?"

"Jason Brown? Late this afternoon, I hope."

"I'd like to meet him."

"I'll be glad to introduce you. Excuse me, there's Mrs. Frothingham!" cried the auctioneer. He rushed away to escort a large, wealthy-looking woman into the tent. Mr. Bunker and Jeff moved away through the crowd.

"I want to take a look at the set-up for our refreshments stand," said Mr. Bunker. "You stay here and keep an eye on things."

Jeff was admiring an old Civil War rifle when a loud crash made him jump. It made everybody else in the crowd jump too. The crash came from near the front of the tent. Like everyone else, Jeff moved in that direction. Being tall, he was able to see what had happened.

Wolfe was standing by one of the tables looking embarrassed. A tall and ugly old-fashioned umbrella stand had been displayed on the table. The stand was made of a shiny brown-colored pottery. It had fallen over into a box of dishes behind the table. The heavy umbrella stand and most of the dishes were smashed to pieces.

"I'm sorry, Mr. Ransom, it's all my fault," Wolfe was saying. "I was terribly clumsy. I knocked that stand over with my elbow. I'll be glad to pay whatever you decide it was worth. The dishes, too."

Hadley Ransom quickly inspected the damage. He gave Wolfe a soothing glance.

"It's not too bad, Mr. Wolfe. Luckily that umbrella stand was worth very little, and the dishes were just kitchen stuff. I put them in a box as an odd lot."

He named a small amount of money. Wolfe insisted on rounding it off to ten dollars. While this was going on, Jeff suddenly remembered Mrs. Walling. She was not there with Wolfe.

He caught his breath.

What a chance for a purse-snatcher or a pickpocket! While everyone else's attention was distracted!

He looked around wildly for her. At that moment she came through the crowd and joined Wolfe.

"Gus, was that you making all that racket?" she asked.

Jeff was glad to see she still had her purse. That was something, at least. But did it prove anything? A clever pickpocket could have taken the necklace out of her purse while the crash was distracting her attention!

"Yes," Wolfe replied to her, pink in the face. "It was me—a bull in a china shop. I knocked over that umbrella stand."

Mrs. Walling inspected the wreckage.

"Well, I think you showed very good taste," she declared, and everybody laughed.

Everybody except Jeff. He was too busy worrying. It was funny that Wolfe had been the one to knock over the stand. What if he had done it on purpose, to give somebody else a chance to . . .

Mr. Tuttle!

Where was Mr. Tuttle?

8

_____

JEFF craned his neck over the crowd, but saw no sign of Mr. Tuttle.

He decided to find Mr. Bunker in a hurry. He slipped outside to the refreshments stand.

"Well, Jeff! What was all that racket?"

Jeff told him what had happened.

"And Mr. Tuttle's gone," he added.

Mr. Bunker turned pale.

"I wanted to go straight to Mrs. Walling and ask her if her necklace was safe," said Jeff, "but I couldn't very well do that. Especially when Wolfe was standing there with her."

Mr. Bunker's jaw set desperately.

"No, but *I'm* going to! This is too much for my nerves! Come on, Jeff—you come along and talk to Wolfe, if they're together, and give me a chance to speak to her."

"What are you going to say to her?"

"I'll just remind her it's dangerous in crowds when something happens to distract everybody's attention. Don't worry, I won't tip our hand about Wolfe."

Wolfe and Mrs. Walling were looking at the Colonial cupboard. Jeff stopped alongside Wolfe.

"Found anything you want to buy, sir?"

Wolfe turned and smiled at him.

"Not so far, Jeff. I bought an umbrella stand I *didn't* want, though."

Jeff managed a small laugh at the fat man's joke on himself.

"I'm glad it wasn't something more expensive."

"So am I."

Jeff talked to Wolfe for another minute, until he saw Mr. Bunker had left Mrs. Walling. Then he excused himself and drifted away after his boss.

"Well?" asked Jeff.

Mr. Bunker was feeling better.

"She squeezed her purse, and then took a look in it, and told me not to be silly. She said the necklace was safe and sound."

"Good! I'm glad that was a false alarm. I wonder where Mr. Tuttle went, though?"

"I don't know and I don't care, so long as that necklace hasn't gone with him!"

Hadley Ransom came along and asked Mr. Bunker a question about soft drink deliveries. They went off to the house together, to look up something in his office. Jeff stayed in the tent to keep an eye on Mrs. Walling.

He walked around, pretending to look at things some more. After a while he was back at the pictures. He glanced at them, watching the reflection of the crowd in the glass.

Suddenly he stood back and stared at the six old pictures. He had realized something.

One of them was gone.

Jeff blinked. Why should one of them be missing? They were nothing special. They were only printed copies of famous pictures. Why would anyone bother to steal one?

Had someone taken it? Or had it simply been taken down, for some reason—maybe by Ransom himself?

At any rate, Jeff decided, he had better check. He had better let Hadley Ransom know about it at once.

He glanced at Mrs. Walling. She should be safe enough, now that Mr. Bunker had warned her about being careful in a crowd.

Jeff left the tent and rushed over to the house. He hurried in the back door and asked a woman in the kitchen where Mr. Ransom's office was. She pointed the way.

The door of his office was open. Ransom and Mr. Bunker were inside, talking.

"Mr. Ransom!"

The men looked around as Jeff appeared.

"Now what?" said Mr. Bunker.

Jeff told them about the missing picture.

"Did you take it down, Mr. Ransom?"

"No, I didn't, Jeff."

"Well, it's gone."

The auctioneer looked more annoyed than concerned.

"Now, who the devil would take that? Those are only reproductions of some Rembrandt etchings. They're not worth much."

Jeff was as puzzled as the rest of them. Though no student of art, he knew that Rembrandt was one of the most famous artists who had ever lived. As for etchings, they were drawings scratched on metal plates from which copies could be made. Etchings made from Rembrandt's own original plates would be worth a fortune. But according to Hadley Ransom, the missing picture was not an original etching, but only a printed reproduction.

Mr. Bunker stared at Jeff in amazement.

"Good Lord! Do you suppose he took *that*?" he asked.

"Who are you talking about?" asked Ransom sharply.

"Well . . ."

Mr. Bunker carefully shut the door. Then he told Ransom all about their suspicions of Wolfe and Mr. Tuttle.

"And after Wolfe caused that disturbance, Mr. Tuttle was missing," Jeff pointed out. "He was carrying his raincoat. He could easily have hidden a picture that size under it. It wasn't a very big picture."

"All along I've been worrying about Myra's necklace," said Mr. Bunker, "but—"

A crash and clatter from the direction of the tent interrupted him. It startled them all.

"What the devil was *that*?" cried Ransom. He peered out the window. "Come on, let's go out there!"

When they reached the tent, they found Wolfe standing beside a tangle of folding chairs. They were part of a pile stacked in one corner of the tent. Once again he was red in the face. Mrs. Walling was standing beside him, laughing heartily.

"Mr. Ransom, I promise to leave at once!" said Wolfe. "I've done it again. I bumped into these chairs. But at least I didn't do any damage this time."

"We're going back to the inn, Ambrose," said Mrs. Walling. "I want to change my shoes, and then we're leaving for Boston. We'll be back in time for dinner."

Standing behind them, raincoat over his arm, was Mr. Tuttle!

After further apologies from Wolfe, the three left and headed for his car, parked nearby. The men stared after them.

"Are you going to tell Mrs. Walling, and stop her from going with them?" Jeff asked.

Mr. Bunker nodded.

"As soon as they've had time to reach the inn, I'll phone her there."

Ransom turned to Jeff.

"I thought you said Tuttle was missing?"

"He was!"

"That's right," agreed Mr. Bunker.

"Hmm. Well, let's see which picture was taken," said Ransom, and led the way across the tent. He reached the pictures first. He had time to take a look and then glance around at Jeff.

His expression was more than puzzled.

"Jeff, are you sure you feel all right?"

Jeff took a quick look, and got a shock.

None of the pictures was missing!

9

$\mathcal{B}$ut I tell you it *was* gone!" Jeff insisted. "This one was gone!"

"Crazy!" muttered Ransom.

"Mr. Tuttle was missing, and so was the picture!" Jeff snapped his fingers.

"And Wolfe knocked down those chairs! Another distraction! That's too much to be just coincidence. I say Mr. Tuttle took the picture down the first time, and put it back the second time."

Ransom began to look less doubtful.

"Could be!" he admitted. "But what did he do with it in between?"

Ransom took the picture off its hook. He looked at the back panel.

"Hey! These nails have been twisted around. Here's a fresh scratch. The back's been taken off this frame!"

"Then he took something out of it!" said Jeff. "He took it outside—probably to the car—and took something out of it."

Now Ransom was concerned.

"Come on!"

He led the way back to his office. Once there, he quickly removed the back of the picture frame.

"Hmm. Nothing here, of course."

He turned the back around and around, carefully peering into all the edges.

"Wait!"

Opening a drawer in his desk, he took out a pair of tweezers. With great care he reached into one corner of the back of the frame. He pulled loose a tiny ragged triangle of paper. He examined it thoroughly through a magnifying glass.

When he looked up he was excited.

"This is definitely very old art paper. It could be a corner of an old drawing, or an etching—"

Ransom slapped his hand against his forehead.

"Jason Brown!"

The others stared at him.

"What about Jason Brown?"

"One of the things he asked about when he phoned me the other day was those pictures. He said he noticed them listed in our auction catalog. He laughed and said he supposed I was sure they were only reproductions of Rembrandt's work and not original etchings."

"And what did you say?"

"I said of course I was sure. And I *am* sure!"

He turned the picture right side up to show them why he was sure.

"Look at this one. It's obviously printed on new, modern paper."

He pushed the picture out of the frame, and pointed to a line of print that had been hidden by the frame.

"See? Here's the name of the printing firm. It was printed right here in America."

Ransom glared at the picture, thinking. Then his eyes lit up.

"But suppose Brown suspected Colonel Collins had got hold of the real thing somewhere? Suppose Wolfe and Tuttle *knew* he had an original, and knew where he had it hidden? Suppose they knew the colonel had it hidden in the frame *behind* one of the reproductions—this one!"

While he talked, Ransom grabbed the Boston telephone directory and looked up a number. He dialed it rapidly.

In a moment he had been put through to Jason Brown's office at the museum.

"Mr. Brown, please. Hadley Ransom calling . . . What? He's left? He's already on his way down?"

He clapped his hand over the receiver and groaned as he told them the news.

"He left early! Just minutes ago!"

Again Ransom spoke into the phone.

"Well, now, listen, this is urgent. Is your boss coming down here because of a picture? I must know, because we've just had a picture stolen here. I didn't think it was valuable, but . . . Please! I know you wouldn't usually give away your boss's secrets, but this is different!"

For a few tense moments Ransom listened breathlessly. He asked a question or two. His expression changed several times. First he looked amazed. Then shocked. Then angry.

"Thank you," he said finally. "Thank you very much! We'll do what we can here. Good-bye."

His hand was trembling as he put down the receiver. All the amazement and shock and anger he felt were still in his face.

"Jason Brown is after a Rembrandt etching that

was last seen in a Dutch museum twenty-five years ago—when the Nazis looted it during World War II!"

"What!"

"His secretary refused to say why he thought Colonel Collins might have had it, but . . . Well, I know one thing—Collins was in Germany during the war, and after it . . ."

His voice sharpened with alarm.

"Listen, if those two crooks have laid their hands on that etching, it will never get back where it belongs! We've got to catch up with them before they leave the inn!"

Mr. Bunker snatched up the receiver and dialed.

"I'll call Myra and tell her to stall!"

But then his face fell. He swore angrily.

"Line's busy!"

"Well, come on, we can't wait! There's no time to lose!"

They nearly trampled each other getting out of the room. The woman working in the kitchen looked popeyed as they charged through. They exploded into the open.

"Take care of things, Joe!" Ransom yelled at a startled assistant. People stared at them as they pounded past. They leaped into Ransom's big station wagon and he gunned it down the driveway.

It was not until they were tearing along the road at breakneck speed that they stopped to think. Then the cold light of reason began to chill their excitement. Ransom slowed down a little. He and Mr. Bunker eyed each other.

"What are we going to do when we get there?"

Mr. Bunker shrugged.

"I don't know, Hadley."

Ransom looked frustrated.

"We don't have one shred of real evidence. I mean, we don't dare accuse them of anything. We could still be wrong about this whole thing. Suppose we accused them of taking something, and then couldn't prove it. Why, they could sue the pants off us!"

"They could ruin us both," agreed Mr. Bunker.

"We can't take a chance like that, Ambrose."

"You're right. We've both got too much at stake. Anyway, why should we?"

"That's right, why should we? If there *is* an etching, and we get it back, it won't put a dime in our pockets."

"We're just asking for trouble."

"You bet we are, Ambrose!"

But then Hadley Ransom smacked one big fist on the steering wheel.

"Just the same, it burns me up to let them get

away with it! It begins to sound like a real dirty business. You know, Colonel Collins was an odd old bird, the way he kept to himself and all."

"He certainly could have had a few secrets in his life," said Mr. Bunker.

"If he did have that etching, he must have swiped it. If the Nazis had it, then how did he get it? How much does Jason Brown know—or suspect? Well, whatever the story is, that etching ought to go back to where it belongs, to Holland. But instead, those two crooks will sell it to some private collector— the kind who doesn't ask questions! There are plenty of those!"

Mr. Bunker sighed heavily.

"But what can we do?"

"What about Myra?"

"Leave that to me. But even if I stop her from going with them, that won't keep Wolfe and Tuttle from leaving."

"If only we could stall them until Jason Brown gets here!"

"But it'll take him a couple of hours! How can we stall them for two hours?"

They had nearly reached the inn. From a high point on the road they could look ahead and see the house.

"Look! There they are, getting in the car right now!"

"Slow down! No sense in making them suspicious. For that matter, they'll wonder why you're bringing us back to the inn as it is, Hadley."

"Say, that's right. Well, I'll tell them your car wouldn't start."

In the meantime, forgotten in the back seat, Jeff had been thinking, too. And with no more luck than the others. It was all too much guesswork. They didn't even know for sure that Wolfe and Mr. Tuttle *were* crooks. They didn't even know for sure there *was* an etching.

But if there was, and they had stolen it, and were able to leave with it now, then the game was really over.

The perfect crime!

10

Ransom turned up the drive. Mrs. Walling waved to them from the front seat of Wolfe's sedan as they stopped alongside.

"Well! What are you doing here?"

"I had to bring Ambrose home," said Hadley Ransom. "His car won't start."

Mr. Bunker got quickly out of the car.

"Can you hold it a minute? I've got a couple of letters I wish you'd mail in Boston for me."

"Certainly, Mr. Bunker," said Wolfe, looking very relaxed behind the wheel. Mr. Tuttle was sitting in back. His dispatch case was on the seat beside him. He had a prim, smug look on his face that somehow annoyed Jeff enormously. If ever Jeff had seen two men who looked pleased with themselves, it was this pair.

Mr. Bunker hurried toward the house. Jeff watched him anxiously. What was his plan?

"We enjoyed your display, Mr. Ransom," said Wolfe while they waited. His manner was more jovial than ever. "I look forward to attending the auction, and I promise to sit still and not break anything!"

Mr. Bunker stuck his head out of the door of the inn.

"Myra! Telephone for you—long distance."

Mrs. Walling clicked her tongue.

"Oh, wouldn't you know it? I wonder who that could be? I won't take a minute."

Wolfe remained smooth, but he glanced at his watch.

"Yes, do try not to be long, Myra. We really should be on our way, if we're going to get Mr. Tuttle to his meeting comfortably."

"I'll make it snappy," she called over her shoulder.

She disappeared into the house. Wolfe chatted easily with Ransom about various items in the auction. Jeff got out of Ransom's station wagon and stood looking at Wolfe's big sedan. He wished he could think of some way of quietly disabling it. But that was ridiculous, of course.

A couple of minutes ticked by. Then Mrs. Walling came out again, looking disappointed.

"Oh, Gus, I'm so sorry, you'll have to go on without me! That was my cousin Ethel. She wasn't supposed to get here till next week, but she's coming today. She'd never forgive me if I wasn't here to greet her."

It was a reasonable story. Mrs. Walling acted her part very well. Jeff watched carefully to see what Wolfe's reaction would be. The fat man groaned and rolled his eyes up and protested.

"But we can be back here by six at the latest, Myra!"

Still, was it Jeff's imagination, or did Wolfe's protest sound just a tiny bit hollow? Was there a hint of relief showing through? And Mr. Tuttle? Didn't he look more smug than ever?

"No, I'm sorry, Gus, I just can't go. You don't know Ethel. She's—well, she's a little difficult."

"I don't think I'm going to like her," declared Wolfe.

"Dear me," said Mr. Tuttle. "I hate to make you drive me all the way to Boston now, Mr. Wolfe . . ."

Wolfe sighed ponderously.

"Not at all, Mr. Tuttle. I can't let you down now. Well, you might as well move up here with me, as long as Mrs. Walling's not going."

"Yes, yes, of course."

Jeff stepped forward and opened the rear door for Mr. Tuttle. The little man took his dispatch case from the seat and stepped out.

This was it, thought Jeff. They were all set now. So? What was it to him? It was no skin off his nose. The smart thing was to keep out of the whole business. Let them get away with it. Just because Mr. Tuttle looked like a little smart alec who had pulled a fast one, Jeff shouldn't let it bother him.

Even as he was thinking these safe, sensible thoughts, something happened inside Jeff. He got mad.

"No, sir!" he shouted angrily.

And snatching the dispatch case away from Mr. Tuttle, he started running!

11

$\mathcal{B}$EHIND him, shouts filled the air. Mrs. Walling screamed. But her scream was nothing compared to the hoot Mr. Tuttle let out. As for Wolfe, he sounded as if he were using a bull horn.

Racing across the lawn, Jeff sped down the path toward the lake.

"*Now* what have I done?" he was thinking.

Maybe there *was* something in the dispatch case. But maybe there were only business papers. Maybe he would end up in jail!

He had let himself be carried away by a lot of wild ideas. Foggy thoughts about justice. About Nazi bullies back in the war, and American crooks right now. All he knew was, at the last instant, he couldn't stand to let them just drive off and get away with it. He had to know the truth, one way or the other.

Now he would be a hunted man.

Turning off the path, he ran into the woods that surrounded most of the lake. He kept going for a while, until he could not hear any shouts behind him. Then he sat down against a tree and stared at the dispatch case.

It had an impressive lock. Not the tin kind most suitcases have. He did not know how to pick locks, anyway. To look inside the case, he would have to force it open.

And that he was not about to do!

Even if Wolfe and Tuttle had stolen an etching, it might not be in the dispatch case. Then where would he be? He had grabbed the case to delay the men. He had not taken it because he felt at all sure the etching was in it. So why break into it? Even if he went to jail, he might get off easier if he had not broken into the case. He knew enough law to know that.

Jeff groaned.

"Man, you've really done it this time!"

He saw himself in a striped suit—broad stripes. For a moment he almost panicked. Then he reminded himself about Jason Brown. He should show up within a couple of hours. The thing to do was to hide out until Brown had time to get there. That was his best chance.

Jeff got to his feet and began to slip through the woods, looking for a good place to hide.

Fifteen minutes later he was under a bush in the thickest patch of underbrush he had been able to find.

The woods were not as thick as he wished they were, but he felt reasonably safe.

Then he heard voices nearby.

He heard voices calling to each other, and the sounds of feet crashing through the underbrush.

"Wow!" muttered Jeff to himself. "Didn't take them long to organize a manhunt!"

Heavy footsteps came nearer. He held his breath.

Rat-a-tat-tat!

He nearly had heart failure. Someone was beating the underbrush with a stick directly over his head! He moved forward, and stared up into the startled eyes of a tall middle-aged man in shorts with a whistle on a cord around his neck.

Jeff sighed. He was not going to add assault and battery to the counts against him.

"Okay, I surrender," he said meekly.

The tall man goggled down at him.

"I beg your pardon?"

"I said, I surrender!"

"You what?"

Jeff gaped up at the man.

"Well, aren't you a—er—what are you, anyway?"

"Why, I'm—I'm a nature study group leader."

"A what?"

"I have a group of teen-agers with me. Boys. Big ones," he added, as if he wanted Jeff to know he had him outnumbered and out-muscled.

Jeff laughed hoarsely. He struggled to his feet and picked up the dispatch case.

"Don't mind me. I'm just a harmless nut," he declared, and walked away as briskly as he could.

He left the group leader with his mouth open. But at least the man didn't start hollering for someone to stop him.

Jeff hurried on through the woods, following a path now. All around him he could hear voices, and the tramp of feet through the underbrush. In fact, some of the group seemed to be straight ahead of him on the path.

Should he stop and hide?

No.

The group leader might have thought things over by now and decided to follow him. He had better keep going.

It would be better simply to act natural, as if he were merely out for a walk. True, he probably looked a little odd, carrying a dispatch case in the woods, but he would have to risk that. He would simply nod pleasantly and say, "Hi," and keep going.

Two teen-agers rounded a bend in the path ahead of him. Jeff nodded pleasantly.

"Hi."

"Hi," said the two boys. They eyed him curiously. No question about it, the dispatch case did make him look funny, out in the woods.

Behind him, the boys had stopped. He was sure they had stopped to watch him. He walked on as briskly as he could without actually breaking into a run.

Somewhere in the distance, up the hill, a siren wailed. A police car, no doubt. Jeff started at the sound, and almost stumbled. He hoped the boys had not noticed.

Once around the bend in the path and out of sight, he began to run. He rounded another bend.

A boy sprang in front of him, his arms spread wide.

"Stop!"

12

$\mathcal{J}$EFF's first impulse was to push the kid in the face and keep going.

Just in time, the boy spoke.

"We're trying to take a picture! Hold it a minute, or he'll fly away!"

Jeff caught himself in time. No boy had ever come closer to getting a push in the face than this one.

"Who'll fly away?" he asked.

"The Great Spangled Fritillary!"

"The what?"

"The butterfly!" said the boy scornfully.

"Oh!"

Jeff peered past him. Crouched beside the path was another boy with a camera. He had it trained on a butterfly sitting on a low bush.

Glancing back over his shoulder, Jeff fidgeted.

"Gee, I'm in a hurry. I—er—I have to get to a meeting. Could you speed it up a little?"

"Listen, you can't speed up nature photography. It takes patience. Just a minute! . . . Okay, Eddie?"

"Naw, Buzzy! He won't open his wings!"

Buzzy glanced back at Jeff and shrugged.

"You see? You can't hurry nature pictures."

"Now, listen, I have an appointment—"

The camera clicked.

"Got it! Okay, Buzzy!"

Buzzy nodded sharply to Jeff.

"Okay."

He stepped aside. But he continued to stare hard at him.

"Okay," said Jeff. He hurried past Buzzy and the crouching Eddie, who also gave him and his dispatch case a funny look.

Jeff was beginning to hate nature. He glared at the Great Spangled Fritillary as it fluttered away down the path ahead of him.

In the distance he could hear sirens. For a seashore town, Westham seemed to have plenty of cops!

He left the path for the woods. From now on he would have to pit his skill as a woodsman against the world—and he was not much of a woodsman. Jeff was not even sure which side of a tree the moss grew on.

Furthermore, he did not know the area he was in. He wished he had been at the inn a little longer, so that he knew what sort of places were around the lake.

Not far ahead, through the trees, he saw what looked like a dense growth. He headed that way, and quickly got caught on some brambles.

"Ouch! Ouch! Ouch!" he muttered as he picked himself loose. Now he was sure he hated nature.

Next he heard water running. A stream was somewhere nearby. In a moment he found himself on the edge of a small brook. Small, but much too large to jump across. Still, once over the brook and into the dense woods, he should be safe. Or safer, at any rate. At least he had not met any more of those nature students. He hoped he had seen the last of them.

He walked along the bank of the brook, looking for a place to cross.

This time a man and woman appeared. They appeared to be regular tourist types. She had on a huge straw hat, and he was wearing a Hawaiian shirt. They were arguing about where they would eat dinner that night. Trying to look at ease, Jeff strolled past them. They scarcely glanced at him.

The brook wound to the right. Dead ahead, he saw an old mill. Too late he realized he was heading straight for a tourist attraction, with lots of people around! It was right on a road, too!

At the same time, however, he saw a ford in the brook. It was just a few yards farther on. There were stones that he could walk on to cross the brook.

He took a chance and kept going to the ford. He started across.

He had hardly taken two steps when he heard brakes screech. His head jerked in the direction of the sound.

A police car had stopped on the road.

The sight was enough to make him lose his balance.

"Yi-i!" cried Jeff, and slipped off a rock. He went into the water up to his knees.

Scrambling out of the brook, he ran wildly back the way he had come. Too late he wished he had waded toward the other bank.

Now he would have to be careful to stay clear of the nature group. If he could only find a thicket to hide in, maybe he could still stall for time. He padded along the path with water squirting out of his shoes.

Behind him he heard a sharp whistle. A police whistle! They were coming after him. He looked around for a place to hide, any place.

At the other side of a small clearing off to his right were some bushes. He hurried toward them. But even as he neared them, he changed his mind.

He might be caught at any moment now. Was he going to let himself be taken with the dispatch case, and not even know if anything really was in it?

If the etching was in it, he was all right.

Jeff glanced around. All was peaceful. A bird chirped somewhere in the underbrush. Now was the time! He sat down in the small clearing, and began to search his pockets for something with which to force open the dispatch case.

A whistle seemed to split his eardrums.

"Grab him, boys!" cried a familiar voice. The voice of the nature study group leader.

Teen-agers seemed to spring out of the ground all around him. He went down under a heap of them. Another whistle sounded. Heavy feet pounded up.

"Officer, there's your man!" cried the group leader.

"Where?"

"Well, he's under there somewhere. Get up, boys, and let this officer take charge!"

13

THE officer was Constable Caleb Hodge of the Westham Police Department. He said so.

He stared grimly at Jeff.

"You Jeff Adams?"

"Yes, sir."

"Here's his bag," said one of the boys. He held up the dispatch case.

"I'll take charge of that there," said Constable Hodge. "He stole it."

"He did? Gee!"

"Come on, Adams," said Constable Hodge. "I'm taking you back to the inn."

Jeff shrugged. The game was up.

"All right, Constable. Let's go."

They started back along the path. The whole nature study group tagged along at their heels.

"I thought he looked suspicious when I first saw him, Constable," the group leader declared proudly. "We followed him, and when he turned back we set a trap for him. He was no match for our woodsmanship!"

"That was good work," said Constable Hodge. "Well, here's the path up to the inn. I'll take him from here."

The nature group let out a group groan.

"Aw, can't we come too?"

"We want to see what happens!"

"Better not to have such a crowd when we get to the inn," said Constable Hodge, speaking to the group leader.

"You heard the officer, boys," said the group leader, even though he sounded disappointed himself. "We can't all go trooping up there."

Leaving the disappointed group behind, Constable Hodge told Jeff to walk ahead of him up the path.

"And don't try to get away, if you don't want to get a leg shot off," he warned sternly.

"You're not fooling me. You don't want the boys to come along because you want to take all the credit," Jeff felt like saying. But he didn't. It wouldn't have been the smartest thing to do, under the circumstances.

As they mounted the path to the inn, Jeff hung his head in despair. Jason Brown would never arrive in time to be of any help now. Maybe he wouldn't be of any help, anyway, but it would be nice to know.

When they reached the lawn at the top of the hill, Constable Hodge shouted ahead toward the inn.

"Hey, Ambrose! I got him!"

He sounded very pleased with himself.

People seemed to pour out of the inn. Mr. Bunker. Hadley Ransom. Mrs. Walling. Old Mrs. Haney. And, of course, Wolfe and Mr. Tuttle, both of them looking ready to kill him on the spot.

Mr. Tuttle rushed forward. He all but dragged the dispatch case out of the constable's grasp.

"Thank you, officer, thank you! Take this young scoundrel away, and charge him with anything you like, I don't care! He's already made me late for my meeting!"

As he talked he was examining the case with an eagle eye.

"Well, thank heavens! It seems to be all right. Mr. Wolfe, I must leave at once!"

Mr. Bunker and Hadley Ransom were staring at Jeff speechlessly. They looked as if they wanted to help, but could not think of anything to do. Ruby came over and nuzzled his hand. He patted her head sadly.

Mr. Tuttle had pulled out his wallet. He took out a large bill.

"Here, officer, I want you to have this. No, no, I insist! I can't thank you enough. These papers are very important to me. I don't know what got into this young idiot. I can't imagine why he took my case," he declared, shooting a hard glance at Jeff with eyes that had become very small. "But at any rate, may I leave now?"

Constable Hodge hesitated, charmed by the feel of the large bill that had been thrust into his hand. "Well . . ."

All at once Jeff saw a final straw to grasp at.

"Wait a minute! This dispatch case is evidence, isn't it, officer?"

The constable glared at him. He looked as if he wished Jeff had not reminded him.

"Well . . ." he began.

"Oh, now, look here," Mr. Tuttle snapped impatiently, "since it's my case, and I've got it back, what does it matter? I'm not really interested in charging this young man with anything. I think what he really needs is a doctor. He's crazy! I suggest Mr. Bunker get rid of him, and we let it go at that."

"No, sir," said Jeff stubbornly. "I'm not going to have him claim later on that I took something out of that case. He's got to open it up right now, and make sure everything is there."

Constable Hodge stared at him.

"Boy, you *are* crazy!" he declared. "If this gentleman is satisfied, and don't want to prefer charges against you, you better let bad enough alone!"

Now Hadley Ransom stepped forward. The expression on his face was beautiful. It was full of understanding.

"Now, hold on, Caleb. Jeff's right. Mr. Tuttle should check the contents of his bag right now."

Mr. Tuttle drew himself up haughtily.

"I'll do nothing of the kind. The papers in this case are of an extremely confidential nature. I wouldn't think of showing them to *anyone*. Besides, it's perfectly obvious the case has not been opened."

"Maybe he picked the lock," suggested Ransom.

Mr. Tuttle gave him a pitying smile.

"Not that lock. It's a very special lock," he declared. "And now, if you'll excuse me . . ."

Hadley Ransom said something under his breath

to Mrs. Walling. She looked surprised, but she reached up and took a hairpin out of her hair. Jeff saw it glint as she gave it to Ransom.

The auctioneer glanced at Jeff. His eyes glittered with a reckless look.

"Jeff! Ambrose! Keep them busy!" he said.

And darting forward, he snatched the dispatch case out of Mr. Tuttle's hand and ran!

Hadley Ransom did not run as far as Jeff had. He ran only a few yards down the driveway.

Jeff leaped forward to get in the way of the opposition and give him time. He found he had some good help.

Ambrose Bunker grabbed Mr. Tuttle around the middle and held on. That left Jeff free to butt Wolfe in the stomach. As for Constable Hodge, for an instant he was stunned. Then he started to move forward, when Mrs. Walling kicked him smartly in the shin.

"You keep out of this," she ordered. It did not take her long to decide which side she was on.

"Ruby, stop it!" cried Mr. Bunker. Ruby was trying to help by grabbing a trouser leg. Unfortunately she had grabbed her master's by mistake.

From Hadley Ransom's direction came a snap. The snap of a lock opening.

"There we are!" He tossed aside the hairpin. "Lucky I had a wild childhood."

Ransom raised the lid of the case. Then he glanced around.

"Well, Mr. Tuttle! And since when is an original Rembrandt etching part of your business papers?"

Mr. Tuttle tore himself loose from Mr. Bunker's relaxed grip. He glared at Hadley Ransom.

"That happens to be one of my prized possessions. I never travel without it. And I'd like to see you prove differently. Ransom, I'm going to sue you for everything you've got!"

"Want to bet?" said Ransom. He held up the etching and pointed to one corner. "Want to bet I can't match this torn corner with a little piece of paper from the back of a certain picture frame? You shouldn't have been in quite as big a hurry when you took it out."

He turned to Constable Hodge. The constable was hopping around on one foot, groaning as he nursed his shin.

"Stop dancing around, Caleb, and take charge of some *real* crooks!"

Wolfe was panting, trying to get back his breath. Now he seemed to swell up like a frog. He exploded in Tuttle's direction.

"You clumsy fool!"

14

$\mathcal{J}$ASON BROWN was a slender gray-haired man with deep-set eyes. It was he who answered most of their questions, later in the day.

"After World War II, I was part of a special group," he explained. "We were assigned the job of recovering art treasures looted by the Nazis. Colonel Collins was a member of the group, too.

"We found everything that was missing from that Dutch museum except for one Rembrandt etching. Long afterward I realized he had a chance to take it before we junior officers knew about it, if it was there. But by then I couldn't have proved anything.

"When I received your auction catalog, Mr. Ransom, I thought there might be a chance the etching would show up among his possessions. Not much of a chance, but still worth coming down for a look around."

"But how did Wolfe know about the etching?" asked Ransom.

"I suspect we'll find he is or has been an art dealer—maybe involved in shady deals before. Sometime or other Colonel Collins must have showed him his prize. Few people can resist showing a possession like that to *somebody*. Maybe he was even thinking of selling it, with Wolfe's help, when he died suddenly.

"When Wolfe learned of his death, and found out about the auction, he saw his big chance. No doubt he intended simply to buy the reproductions at the auction. He could have had them for a few dollars, and no one the wiser as to what he was really buying.

"When he heard I was coming, however, he decided to take no chances. The colonel had probably told him about the group we both worked with, and mentioned my name. There was an outside chance I might be on the trail of the missing etching. So Wolfe decided to make sure of it beforehand.

With Tuttle's help, he could get his hands on it before I showed up. And I must say, his plan was a dandy. It should have been foolproof."

"It still would have worked, if Jeff hadn't grabbed that case," said Ambrose Bunker.

He turned to Jeff.

"Why did you do it?"

Jeff shrugged. He felt downright embarrassed. How could he explain? He hardly knew himself.

"You heard what Mr. Tuttle said. I'm crazy!"

As they all laughed, he glanced at Hadley Ransom.

"For that matter, why did *you* do it?"

Ransom grinned.

"Oh, I couldn't let you take *all* the risks!"

"Well, whatever your reasons," said Jason Brown, "you did the Dutch government a big favor. This etching is one of their national treasures. They'll probably want to give you both a medal."

"What about Mr. Bunker?" said Jeff. "It all started because he was suspicious of Wolfe."

"I was right about him for the wrong reasons," said Mr. Bunker. "For that matter, what about Myra? She ought to get a medal for kicking Constable Hodge in the shin. I've wanted to do that for years."

Mrs. Walling laughed. She opened her purse and

took out her diamond necklace. It flashed fire as she twirled it gently.

"And to think it all started because Ambrose was worried about this! Well, I don't really need it here, Ambrose. Tomorrow I'll put it away in a safe deposit box, and then you can relax. These diamonds have caused enough trouble."

Mr. Bunker laughed dryly.

"If you asked Wolfe and Tuttle," he said, "I'll bet they'd agree!"

ABOUT THE AUTHOR

SCOTT CORBETT, author of *The Cave Above Delphi* and *Pippa Passes,* has written for adults as well as for young people, but he is perhaps best known for his widely popular, highly successful mysteries for young readers —among them *Tree House Island, Dead Man's Light,* and *Cutlass Island,* which won the 1962 Edgar Allan Poe Award given by the Mystery Writers of America for the best mystery for children each year.

Most of DIAMONDS ARE TROUBLE was written while Mr. Corbett and his wife were traveling around the world on freighters last year—but the setting is based on an inn on Cape Cod in Massachusetts. When they are at home, the Corbetts live in Providence, Rhode Island.

96.